The Nearly Ghost Baby

DELIA HUDDY

Illustrated by
DAVID WILLIAM

PUFFIN BOOKS

CHILLERS

The Blob Tessa Potter and Peter Cottrill
Clive and the Missing Finger Sarah Garland
The Day Matt Sold Great-grandma Eleanor Allen and Jane Cope
The Dinner Lady Tessa Potter and Karen Donnelly
Ghost from the Sea Eleanor Allen and Leanne Franson
Hide and Shriek! Paul Dowling
Jimmy Woods and the Big Bad Wolf Mick Gowar and Barry Wilkinson
Madam Sizzers Sarah Garland
The Mincing Machine Philip Wooderson and Dee Shulman
The Real Porky Philips Mark Haddon
Sarah Scarer Sally Christie and Claudio Muñoz
Spooked Philip Wooderson and Jane Cope
Wilf and the Black Hole Hiawyn Oram and Dee Shulman

PUFFIN BOOKS

Published by the Penguin Group
Penguin Books Ltd, 27 Wrights Lane, London W8 5TZ, England
Penguin Books USA Inc., 375 Hudson Street, New York, New York 10014, USA
Penguin Books Australia Ltd, Ringwood, Victoria, Australia
Penguin Books Canada Ltd, 10 Alcorn Avenue, Toronto, Ontario, Canada M4V 3B2
Penguin Books (NZ) Ltd, 182–190 Wairau Road, Auckland 10, New Zealand

Penguin Books Ltd, Registered Offices: Harmondsworth, Middlesex, England

First published by A&C Black (Publishers) Ltd 1996
Published in Puffin Books 1997
3 5 7 9 10 8 6 4

Text copyright © Delia Huddy, 1996
Illustrations copyright © David William, 1996
All rights reserved

The moral right of the author and illustrator has been asserted

Filmset in Meridien

Made and printed in England by William Clowes Ltd, Beccles and London

Chapter One
The House on the Hill

We first saw the house as we came out of the dip and rounded the bend in the lane down to the beach. The corner was sharper than Dad realised. He wasn't ready for it and almost hit the opposite bank. Not that it mattered, there was never any traffic in the lane. Only we didn't know that then.
Sparks flew. Mum screeched:

Bob! Do be CAREFUL!

WHOOPS!

Having just driven the best part of 300 miles, my dad was on a pretty short fuse. But he ground his teeth to stop himself answering back. Carey was with us and he had to be polite in front of a guest.

Anyway, there was the house, half-way up the hill. The sun was getting low and cast a red glow over the bricks. It seemed warm and friendly-looking. When I saw the two windows in the roof squinting out to sea like eyes, I immediately shouted:

Mum hesitated. "Do you think this is it? It looks awfully big – not really a cottage . . ."

Dad said there wasn't anywhere else and, besides, he for one didn't feel like driving any further. There was certainly no other cottage in sight – only the beach below, its sand all brown and smooth from the tide going out and just asking for footprints.

There wasn't a soul about. Mum noticed from the moment we arrived how lonely it was but Carey and I didn't. We were out of the car almost before it stopped.

Dad shouted after us. But we didn't take blind bit of notice. Poor Dad!

It was great to be there after all that time cramped up in a sweltering car – three quarters of it taken up by Brian and his baby paraphernalia.

We wrenched
off our trainers.
Then we dashed across the sand and put
our toes in
the sea.

Yikes!
It's cutting
cold.

Eeeeek!

Chapter Two
Carey

I'd better explain what we were doing in Cornwall instead of lazing on a sunny beach in Spain or Greece – and, of course, why Carey was with us. I can't remember exactly when she took a shine to me. It must have been soon after Brian was born.

Brian was red-headed (not red-haired – he didn't have any!), red-faced, red-eyed and I thought altogether yukky. Our family had been perfectly OK with just the three of us – me, Mum and Dad.

The day Mum came to meet me after school, proudly pushing the pram, Carey immediately hung over it making stupid noises . . .

Like some old granny

Glur-lurg. Ugll-ll-it-itty, pitty-itty. Ooo, he's lovely Mrs Carter! Can I push him just a little way? I'll be careful. Oh, look at his little button nose....

Of course Mum said, "What a nice friend for you, Lisa," and asked Carey to tea.

On that Saturday, the choice was to go swimming with Dad, or to watch Brian having his bath. You can guess what I wanted to do. And you can guess what Carey wanted.

I asked angrily as she skipped after Mum who was carrying Brian to the bathroom.

I watched *Skyraiders* in disgust.

Mum said she was going to ask Carey's mother if Carey could come on holiday with us to Cornwall.

It'll be nice for you to have a friend there.

Not that WALLY!

Mum said I didn't deserve to go on holiday if I talked like that about people.

Well, I didn't want to go to Cornwall and I didn't want Carey to come. For as long as I could remember, every summer we had gone to Portugal, or Greece, or Minorca – somewhere where it was lovely and hot.

But Brian was even spoiling our holidays now! Mum said he was too tiny to take on a plane, and he needed so much luggage.

And, as if I was six, Dad said, "Just think! Celts live in Cornwall – the most ancient people in Britain. . ."

At first I said:

But later I changed my mind. Someone I didn't really like was probably better than *no one* at all on a cold beach in the rain.

Chapter Three
Sun and Sandcastles

Carey and I slept in the attic. It ran the width of the roof – one long wide room with two flights of stairs leading up to it. The back stairs came up to our bedroom on the left and the bigger front stairs, with a proper landing, on the right. My bed was by the door to the back stairs.

Carey bagged the bed along the front wall (she would!). She could kneel up and look out right over the whole bay.

It was a funny old house – very bare, with only a few bits of enormous, heavy furniture. It didn't feel at all lived in. You wouldn't think people had been there for holidays off and on all summer.

And no trace of a telly! Dad said every holiday cottage had a telly these days and what did the people think they were letting? Who were they anyway? He would ring them up. Mum seemed vague about them. There had only been a box number to write to in the Sunday paper.

But Dad forgot about the TV because the first three days were so hot and sunny we were outside all the time. Really *grand*.

We ran down the track through an amazingly tangly garden full of ticking crickets and straight on to the sand!

In fact, I have to admit Cornwall was everything Mum had said it would be and I forgot about missing Greece or Spain.

The sun never went in. There it was when we woke up, climbing from behind the hill; and when we went to bed it was setting over the sea in a great greeny-yellow blob.

We spent the whole time on the beach. It was all blue sky and blue sea – and the sand was brilliant for making castles. Dad was a star at building huge fortifications that we stood on as the tide came in.

We poked around for hours in the rock pools with nets on sticks but never caught anything.

Even Brian didn't cry so much and Mum rigged up a sunshade on the pram.

Carey was still besotted. I will say that for her, she was faithful to Brian.

On the third day we found the cave.

Chapter Four
The Cave

We found it
when we were on
the shady side of the beach.
We were messing about in the rock pools
at the bottom of the steep cliff when Carey
gave a sudden shriek. I wasn't too excited
because she shrieked at most things.

She was right. And that was the moment
everything changed.

We scrambled up over a patch of shaly
cliff to a small dark opening.

I beckoned to him with swirling arms.

He shouted, "Hold on, I'm coming," and
he leaped over the rocks towards us.

I said and pulled a silly face at Dad.

"Carey found it," I said, thinking she would be pleased to have the credit.

But she only said:

By this time Dad was right inside.

I was already off back down the cliff.

By the time I got back with the torch, Dad had been all round the cave and found what he thought might be a passage at the back. Carey was still hopping around in the entrance like the weed she was.

I could see he didn't want to leave her on the rocks by herself. Mum had already gone back to the house to feed Brian.

"We might get trapped," Carey insisted.

Dad said, "No way. Tide's still going out. We've got a good hour before it even turns. Keep the light low, Lisa, so we can see where we're putting our feet."

Actually, Carey was right. There was an overpowering smell of salty seaweed but stronger than that was a sweeter smell – kind of musty and a bit sickly.

And there *was* a passage. It wasn't long before it started going uphill. I led the way. "Steps," I said, my voice all squeaky. "Going up . . ."

The steps climbed more steeply. Up and up. They not only got steeper, they got narrower too.

Carey kept on whinging but Dad squeezed
her hand and said cheerfully, "We'll be out
on the top before you can say *torch* . . ."

25

If I'm honest, I wasn't liking it much either. Down in the cave with the sunlight just outside, it had been exciting. But now, thick darkness had closed in and I thought of the earth below and above and around us and the little crack which was the steps we were climbing up.

What if it moved – slid in and crushed us? We'd all be just another bit of earth, like a long layer of squidgy plasticine.

Even though Dad was right behind me, I began to go slower and slower. Then I stopped.

It was the stub of a candle, an old greasy bit of wax on the step. All of a sudden the passage wasn't just ours, it was someone else's too. Other people had been up and down. Did they still use it?

Carey tried to tug her hand out of Dad's.

Let's go back.

Hang on, Hang on, we must be nearly at the top.

The stairs turned slightly to the right. I was watching where I put my feet in the torchlight when, suddenly, I hit my head on something – something wooden.

Then, just as I lifted the torch to see if there was a door knob, I *felt* something – something frightening. And, I *heard someone sigh*.

But it wasn't Carey. She was behind Dad and at least three steps below me. The sigh had been close to my ear. I clutched hold of Dad as he reached past me, saying, "Let's see."

"Huh," said Dad. "Mind out," and he put a hefty shoulder against the door. It didn't give an inch. He straightened up and I knew he was thinking.

I felt cold – very, very cold. The cold in the stairway suddenly became icy, like it might if you walked into a freezer cupboard. Goose pimples crawled up my legs.

As nobody was making a sound, I said angrily, "We're not exactly—" but Dad hissed, "Sshh!" again sharply.

In the silence I could hear my heart
pounding. Then I heard what *he* had
heard – quite thinly, but there all right.
The sound of a baby crying.

"Brian!" It was the first time I'd
ever been glad to hear him.

"What did I tell you," Dad said,
"we're at the house!"

Carey started
shouting wildly.

Dad and I joined in.

Get a move on!

Hurry up Mum!

It seemed for ever but it was probably only a minute or two before someone began rattling the door from the other side.
A key grated, stuck, grated again.

We rushed forward and found ourselves at the bottom of the back stairs. I wondered why we hadn't noticed the door from inside. We must have assumed it was just a cellar. Dad locked it and put the key in his pocket.

Of course we had to explain it all to Mum, who said:

A real smugglers' passage.

And she looked excited and bothered all at the same time.

"Don't worry, you won't catch me going down there," said Carey, and I knew we wouldn't.

Dad told me to stop being silly. So I shut up because what's the good of saying things when people just get mad at you? But the holiday was never the same after that.

Chapter Five
An Old Photograph

In the afternoon the sun went in. By
supper-time a fog was creeping up over
the beach. Dad said the fog came in with
the tide but it kept rolling right
up the hill to the house –
and then rolled over it.
It was a real chiller.

"Sea fret," Dad called it when we went to
bed. "After all this hot weather. It'll be
gone by morning."

He was wrong. It was still there next day and a foghorn had started mooing like a cow further down the coast, making everything seem extra creepy. Dad said we might as well go into Penzance which was only half an hour's drive away.

He does think of some soppy things. But we went along with him and drew moustaches on our faces with charcoal from the fire.

Penzance was full of pirates, parking cars, strolling round the harbour, and buying crab shells and painted pebbles.

Mum looked rather odd with a small pirate
fast asleep in his sling bag.

Carey wanted a postcard to send home but couldn't find one with fog on it. While we were waiting for her to choose, Dad twizzled the stand with the paperbacks on local history. Suddenly he said loudly:

And it was. There was an old photograph taken over a hundred years ago. Our house against the hill. But there were other cottages there too, above and below. It was part of a village.

Dad read out what it said in the book. *"At the end of the nineteenth century, there was a fishing village at one end of Carndower Bay with over a dozen houses. But on the night of December 12 1907, a huge storm damaged the cottages and wiped out the entire fishing fleet. All the men of the village were drowned."*

Mum said, "How terrible. No wonder the house seems sad."

"*Over the next few years,*" Dad read on, "*the womenfolk gradually moved away. The houses fell into disrepair and eventually most of them collapsed . . . .* All except ours! It must have been sheltered there against the hill."

We didn't know whether we felt better or worse to know about the storm and the awful fate of the fishermen in our bay.

Chapter Six
A Warning

On the way home we stopped at the village shop.

We all trooped in. Behind the Post Office counter, a lady with her hair drawn back in little tightly-rolled grey sausages was counting out some change for an old gentleman. He must have been deaf – she was talking very loudly.

He turned round and looked at us, then spoke loudly to Mrs Sausage-Rolls.

She spoke quietly as if she felt awkward with the old man talking about us like that.

I wondered how she knew who we were.
But she'd got it wrong. I piped up and said
almost as loudly as
the old man:

We're staying at Beach House.

The woman said, "It's called *Widows*
really," and she looked embarrassed.

The man's eyes were red-rimmed and
watery as they are when people get very
old. He stared thoughtfully at us.

When the old man said that, Carey gasped and I felt very peculiar. I know now what people mean when they say their legs turned to jelly. Mine did just that.

48

George looked at Brian and asked Mum:

Then he picked up his money and shuffled out slowly, shaking his head.

Mum laughed nervously. "Old local legend, I suppose?" she said to the woman.

But Mrs Sausage-Rolls looked rather uncomfortable and just said:

Dad leaned on the counter.

Mrs S-R busied herself tidying the stamps and Dad said, "What a tragedy to have the fishing fleet washed away."

Those were hard times.

Dad wasn't going to be put off.

Must have been a colourful bit of coast. Known for its smuggling wasn't it?

Mrs S-R nodded. Then Carey butted in.

We found a passage! It goes from the house down to a cave on the beach and it's HORRIBLE!

"Well I never!" Mrs S-R exclaimed, but she didn't really look surprised.

Dad asked Mrs S-R if people in the village knew about the passage and reluctantly she said, "Oh yes, but they don't ever go there. No one goes to that house. No one knows who owns it or anything about it." She gave us a funny look.

Dad wanted to know if it was often let to summer visitors and Mrs S-R told him never as far as she could remember.

And what about the ghost?

Mrs S-R seemed even less keen on telling us about that. She dropped something on the floor, got off her stool and spent a long time picking it up.

In the end she gave a sigh and said, "It's supposed to be a young woman who lived there. When her husband was drowned in the storm she couldn't get over it. She used to go down to the cave with their baby and look out for him, as if he would come wading in out of the sea. It must have turned her mind, the grief of it all."

"And then one day when she was down there, a great wave roared in and swept the baby out of her arms, so she lost that too. It's said her spirit can't rest and she haunts the house!"

Chapter Seven
Ghost in the Night

That conversation was enough to give anyone the jim-jams. We had a great old argument with Dad and Mum. I said, "Well I felt her in the passage, didn't I?" They said again it was just imagination, that there weren't such things as ghosts anyway, and the Cornish always were great ones for making up stories.

Mum cooked my favourite supper of baked potatoes, baked beans and sausage, then we played a game of demon patience. For once, they didn't tell me to stop shrieking because it would wake Brian. They were trying hard to take our minds off ghosts.

But when we went to bed, I put a chair against the door to the back stairs. I don't know what good I thought it would do, because surely ghosts can pass *through* anything. Carey dropped off quite quickly and I suppose I eventually fell asleep too.

Suddenly, I was awake! I could see Carey's outline in the patchy moonlight. The fog had cleared. Everything came back to me. I held my breath I was so frightened. I could feel and hear the chair moving rather than see it.

People say they *nearly died of fright* and I honestly thought I would. I kept saying to myself through chattering teeth, "Ghosts don't move chairs. They can just come *through* closed doors."

But the chair fell over and the door swung open with its usual C-R-E-E-A-K.

A cold, strong draught blew in.
I could feel the coldness even though
I had buried myself under the bedclothes.

I wanted to scream, I wanted to shout to Carey to wake up. I wanted to run to Mum and Dad. But I couldn't move. I couldn't make a sound. I was stiff – petrified! The only thing I didn't want to do was *look*.

Something was in the room, I knew it.

Was it the *thing* that lurked in the stairway down to the cave? From under the duvet, I heard the door open on to the landing at the other end of the room. And I heard a great sigh, only it was more like a sob this time. I thought, I'll never move again. I'll stay perfectly still until morning when Mum comes in. Then I heard Brian cry.

WAGH-WAGH-WAGH-WAGH

Suddenly it flashed into my mind – the old man in the Post Office saying:

...Mind the ghost don't get him.

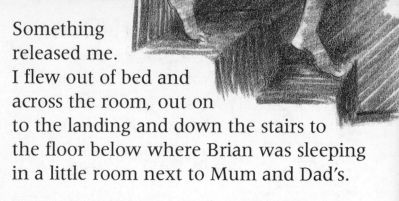

Something
released me.
I flew out of bed and
across the room, out on
to the landing and down the stairs to
the floor below where Brian was sleeping
in a little room next to Mum and Dad's.

I just about fell down the stairs I was in
such a panic. Then I *saw her!* She was
bending over the cot to lift Brian out. He
was really wailing now and thrashing his
arms about.

I screamed:

I threw myself at her just as she took him in her arms. In those few seconds she turned to face me in the light that was now coming from Mum's room. Her look was so tragic, so sad, so *pleading*. I had never seen a face like hers. But I snatched Brian from her and she sort of . . . melted, vanished away. Brian was cold as ice.

Mum switched the light on and of course there was a great deal of explaining to do. Dad insisted I'd had a bad dream because of the old man in the Post Office and that my imagination was too vivid by half.

"IMAGINE THAT FACE!" I was shaking. "I-I-I c-couldn't have imagined it if I had tried for a hundred years. It was there, in front of me . . ."

I've never ever seen such... such sadness!

Then, Mum said very quietly, "Bob, there *was* someone. *I* felt it too! I don't know who it was but she would have taken our Brian if Lisa hadn't stopped her."

"Ahhh!" I slid into a heap on the floor.

Chapter Eight
A Face at the Window

Next day we left to stay on a farm in
North Cornwall for the rest of the holiday.
Carey said she felt homesick and, after a
lot of phone calls, her dad came to get her.

I didn't realise until she'd gone, how glad
I was to be on my own with just Mum
and Dad and Brian. Carey wasn't a *best*
friend – we didn't have real fun together.

And I think Brian knows who I am – now
that Carey isn't around, always making
faces at him. He blinks at me and sort of
screws up his face when I say:

Grr.. rr.. rr
BOO!

And he's got a red haze on
his head which *might* be hair. He
could even turn out to be handsome!

As we were leaving *Widows*, I looked back
at the house. I wish I hadn't.

Someone was standing at the top bedroom
window, watching us go. I closed my eyes
quickly and when I opened them again
the house and the bay were out of sight.
I don't ever want to see that house again.

I buried my face in Brian's smelly babygro
and – you won't believe this, I hardly could
myself – I felt really glad we'd got him.